If your child struggles with a word, you can encourage "sounding it out," but keep in mind that not all words can be sounded out. Your child might pick up clues about a word from the picture, other words in the sentence, or any rhyming patterns. If your child struggles with a word for more than five seconds, it is usually best to simply say the word.

Most of all, remember to praise your child's efforts and keep the reading fun. After you have finished the book, ask a few questions and discuss what you have read together. Rereading this book multiple times may also be helpful for your child.

Try to keep the tips above in mind as you read together, but don't worry about doing everything right. Simply sharing the enjoyment of reading together will increase your child's reading skills and help to start your child off on a lifetime of reading enjoyment!

Frank and the Tiger

A We Both Read® Book

We Both Read® is a trademark of Treasure Bay, Inc.

Published by Treasure Bay, Inc.
P.O. Box 119
Novato, CA 94948 USA

Printed in Singapore

Library of Congress Catalog Card Number: 2011935124

Hardcover ISBN: 978-1-60115-259-6
Paperback ISBN: 978-1-60115-260-2

We Both Read® Books
Patent No. 5,957,693

Visit us online at:
www.WeBothRead.com

PR 11-11

Frank and the Tiger

By Dev Ross

Illustrated by Larry Reinhart

TREASURE BAY

One day, Frank put on an old hat. It looked like a jungle explorer hat, so Frank asked Mikey, "Do you want to look for wild animals with me?"

Mikey answered, . . .

"No!"

Suddenly, they heard a noise. Mikey said, "I hope it's not a lion!"

Then a face peeked through the bushes.

"**It is** not a lion," said Frank.

 "It is a boy!"

The boy called out, "Tiger! Where are you, Tiger?"

"Oh, dear," said Frank. "**He is** looking for his lost tiger."

"He is sad."

Frank did not like seeing the boy so sad. "Let's find his lost tiger for him," he said. And off he went.

Hop, hop, hop!

Mikey did not want to look for a tiger. But what if the tiger wanted to look for Mikey??

Mikey began to **run**, racing to catch up to Frank.

Run, run, run!

Frank spotted something. It looked like a tail.
He crept up quietly to see if **it was** the tiger.

It was not.

Mikey did not want to look for the **tiger** anymore. He wanted to go home. Then suddenly, there it was in front of him.

The **tiger!!!**

Mikey was scared, but Frank was brave. "**Come,** tiger," he said, "we are taking you home."

The tiger did not move. It was a toy!

Now Mikey was brave, too. He said, . . .

"Come, tiger!"

Then they heard loud barking. They turned around to see a **dog** running right towards them! Frank held up his hand and shouted, . . .

"Stop, **dog**, stop!"

The dog did not stop. He **ran** past Mikey and Frank. He picked up the tiger in his mouth and kept running.

He **ran** and ran!

"We have to rescue the tiger!" shouted Frank. "We have to bring him back to the little boy."

Mikey knew that Frank was right.

"**Here** comes the dog again," said Frank.

"And **here** we go!"

Frank grabbed the dog's tail with one hand and Mikey with the other. "**This is** great," said Frank as they were pulled into the air.

 **"This is fun!"**

Frank held tightly to Mikey's hand. Soon Mikey was enjoying the ride, too. He shouted, . . .

 "Yes! It is fun!"

The dog stopped and Frank let go of its tail. Frank grabbed the tiger. "Let go," he told the dog, as he began to **tug**.

Tug, tug, tug!

The dog was strong. "What can we do?" said
Frank. "He won't let go!"

"Your hat," yelled Mikey. "**Throw** your hat, Frank!"

"Throw it!"

Frank threw his hat. It flew through the air like a flying saucer. The dog started to run after it.

Run, dog, run!

Now it was time to take the tiger back to the boy. Frank and Mikey dragged it to his door. Then they heard footsteps. **Was** it the boy?

It **was** the boy!

The boy saw his tiger. He gave it a big hug. Then the big dog came running in. The boy threw the tiger and shouted, . . .

"Go, boy! Get it!"

Frank and Mikey had rescued the tiger from the dog. Now the boy was giving it back to him!

Frank laughed. Mikey laughed too!

It was funny!

"Come on," said Frank. "**Let's go** and rescue the tiger again!"

"Okay," said Mikey.

"Let's go!"

If you liked *Frank and the Tiger,* here is another We Both Read® Book you are sure to enjoy!

Just Five More Minutes!

It's Mark's bedtime, but he begs his mom for "just five more minutes!" When his five minutes are up, he keeps coming up with more things to do that will take him "just five more minutes." Each new thing is more funny and outlandish than the last, including teaching a dinosaur how to tie his shoes and brushing George Washington's teeth on Mount Rushmore!